WUBBZY
AND
The Wubb Girlz

ISBN-13: 978-0-545-19724-3
ISBN-10: 0-545-19724-4

© 2009 Bolder Media, Inc./Starz Media, LLC. All Rights Reserved.

Wow! Wow! Wubbzy! and all related titles, logos and characters are trademarks of Bolder Media, Inc./Starz Media, LLC.
www.wubbzy.com

Published by Scholastic Inc. SCHOLASTIC and associated logos are trademarks and/or registered trademarks of Scholastic Inc.

12 11 10 9 8 7 6 5 4 3 2 1   9 10 11 12 13/0

Printed in the U.S.A.
First printing, August 2009

WUBBZY
AND
The Wubb Girlz

By Sierra Harimann
Illustrated by Frank Rocco

SCHOLASTIC INC.
New York Toronto London Auckland
Sydney Mexico City New Delhi Hong Kong

Choo-choo! **Wubbzy loved watching trains. One day he was at the train station when the Wuzzleburg Express arrived.**

Three girls got off the train. Wubbzy had never seen them before.
"Wow! Wow!" Wubbzy said. "My name is Wubbzy."
"Hi, Wubbzy," said the first girl. "I'm Sparkle."
"I'm Shimmer," said the second girl.
"And I'm Shine!" sang the third.

"Wow! Cool names," Wubbzy said. "Can I show you around Wuzzleburg?"
"That would be awesome!" the girls said.

Wubbzy took them to the Yum! Yum! restaurant.
"Hi, everyone!" Wubbzy said. "These are my new friends—"
"THE WUBB GIRLZ!" everyone shouted.

"Huh?" Wubbzy asked. "Who are the Wubb Girlz?"

"*They* are, little buddy," Widget replied as she motioned to Sparkle, Shine, and Shimmer.

"They're the most famous singing group in the world!" Daizy added.

"We have a special announcement to make," Shine said.

"We're hosting Wuzzleburg Idol, a talent contest right here in Wuzzleburg. The winner gets to perform with us in Wuzzlewood!"

"Wuzzlewood?!" Wubbzy exclaimed. "Wow, wow!"

Wubbzy and his friends couldn't wait for the Wuzzleburg Idol talent show.

Daizy practiced her dance steps. She could move just like the Wubb Girlz.

Walden could play all of the Wubb Girlz' hit songs.

And Widget's Voice Choice 3000 could sing all three Wubb Girlz parts at once!

It seemed like everyone in town could sing and dance just like the Wubb Girlz. Everyone except Wubbzy.

Wubbzy was feeling sad when he saw the Wubb Girlz. "What's wrong, Wubbzy?" Shine asked.

"I can't be in the talent contest because I can't sing or dance like you," Wubbzy told them. "I'll never win the trip to Wuzzlewood!"

The Wubb Girlz giggled.

"Don't be silly!"
Sparkle said.

"You don't have to sing and
dance like us," Shimmer
added.

"You just have to be
yourself!" Shine sang out.

"You're right!" Wubbzy said.

Finally it was time for the Wuzzleburg Idol talent show.
Wubbzy watched all of the performers and cheered.

When it was his turn, Wubbzy played his ukulele, juggled, did bouncy flips, and sang—all at the same time!
He was a big hit.

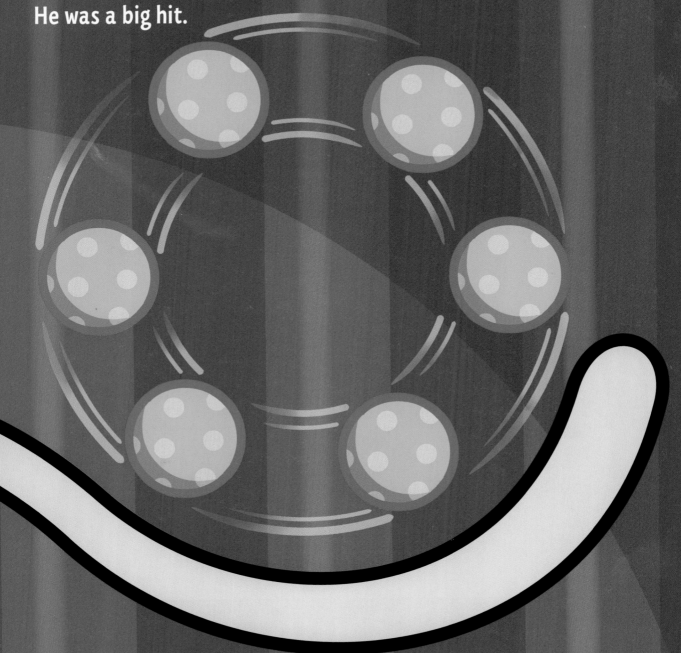

"We're ready to announce the winner," Sparkle began.
"There were so many awesome acts," Shimmer continued.
"But one performer really stood out," Shine concluded.
"The winner of Wuzzleburg Idol is . . ."

"... WUBBZY!"

"Congratulations, Wubbzy," Shine said. "You're going
to perform with us in Wuzzlewood."
"Wow, WOW!" Wubbzy said.
"We'll see you there!" the Wubb Girlz said.

The next day Wubbzy was all set for his big trip to Wuzzlewood. Widget, Walden, and Daizy were coming with him in the Wubbmobile.

"Hey! Lookie there!" Widget exclaimed. "We drive right past Tool Town! Let's stop!"

"Sorry, Widget," Walden said. "It's not on the schedule."

"Come on, Walden," Wubbzy said. "Half the fun of a road trip is enjoying the stops along the way."

Walden checked his watch. "Well, okay," he said reluctantly. "But we can only stop for three minutes."

Widget wanted to stop at the Wrench Restaurant for Hammerburgers and Wrench Fries.

"No, no, no!" Walden said. "Time's up. We have to go."

He pushed everyone back onto the Wubbmobile.

Once they were back on the road, Daizy wanted to
stop in Floweropolis.

Walden shook his head. "It's not on the schedule."

"Come on, Walden," Wubbzy pleaded. "Half the fun of
a road trip is enjoying the stops along the way."

Walden sighed. "Okay, but no stopping," he said.
"Just a quick drive-through."

"Ahhh!" Daizy said. "It smells amazing!"
Wubbzy spotted something in the distance.
"Look!" he exclaimed. "It's Wackyworld, the
greatest amusement park of all time!"

"No, no, no, Wubbzy!" Walden said. "Wackyworld is definitely not on the schedule."

"Aw, Walden," Wubbzy said. "Half the fun—"

"I know, I know," Walden said. "But if we make any more stops, we'll be late to meet the Wubb Girlz in Wuzzlewood!"

Wubbzy was not happy.

"Okay, everybody," Walden announced, "it's time for our five minute stretching break."

While everyone was stretching, Wubbzy snuck out the back door.

"Wackyworld, here I come!" Wubbzy said.

Wubbzy took a ride on the Kooky Coaster.
"Wheeee!" Wubbzy yelled. "Wooooooo! Wowwwww!"
Wubbzy was having the time of his life.

"Whooo-ooh!" Wubbzy shouted. "Which ride should I go on next?"
Suddenly Wubbzy saw three familiar faces. It was the Wubb Girlz!
"What are you doing here?" Wubbzy asked. "I thought you were
going straight to Wuzzlewood!"

"We Wubb Girlz like to have fun, too, you know," Shine said.
"We sure do!" Shimmer and Sparkle added.
"So let's go on the Wacky Parachutes!" Shine shouted.

"This is fun!" Wubbzy said as he landed right in front of Walden.
"Wubbzy! Why did you sneak away like that?" Walden asked. "Now
we'll never make it to Wuzzlewood in time to meet the Wubb Girlz."

"But they're right here!" Wubbzy said.
"But . . . but . . . you're supposed to be in Wuzzlewood!"
Walden protested.
"Wubb Girlz like to have fun, too!" Shine replied.

"Well, in that case, I would like to try that Kooky Coaster," Walden admitted. "Wubbzy, you were right. Half the fun of taking a trip is enjoying the stops along the way."

"Come on," Shine said. "Let's go on some rides! We can all take the Wubbjet to Wuzzlewood later."

Later that day, the Wubbjet landed in Wuzzlewood. The
Wubb Girlz gave Wubbzy and his friends a tour.
"This is the famous Wuzzlewood Boulevard," Shine said.

"Ooo-wee!" Widget exclaimed. "Look at all the shiny cars!"
"Even the sidewalks are sparkly!" Daizy added.
"Wow!" Wubbzy said. "Everything in Wuzzlewood is so fancy."

"And this is the theater where we're doing our concert tonight!
Thousands will be watching us!" Shine said.

"Wow, wow!" Wubbzy said. "*Th-th-thousands?*"

Suddenly Wubbzy's stomach felt like it was full of butterflies.

"What if no one likes me?" Wubbzy said softly.

"You won the Wuzzleburg Idol talent show for being yourself,
so just be yourself tonight," Shine told Wubbzy. "Everyone's going
to love you!"

A few hours later, Wubbzy was waiting backstage.
There were so many people in the audience!
"What if I'm too scared to sing?" he asked Daizy.

"You can do it!" Daizy reassured him. "You just have to believe in yourself. Maybe a new costume will help!"

Daizy gave Wubbzy an outfit. But it was too fluffy.

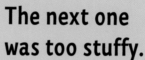 The next one was too stuffy.

The third one was too flashy!

"Here's our star!" Shine said. "Are you ready for the big show?"
"I don't think so," Wubbzy admitted. "I still have stage fright."
"We know all about stage fright," Shimmer said.
"But when we're together, we don't feel as scared," Sparkle said.

"Maybe you'd feel better if you brought your friends onstage with you!" Shine suggested.

"Really?" Wubbzy was thrilled. "They can come onstage with me? That would be great!"

The Wubb Girlz, Wubbzy, and his friends took the stage.
The Wubb Girlz sang their hit song as Wubbzy and his
friends sang backup. The crowd loved it!

As the Wubb Girlz and Wubbzy left the stage, the reporter Jann Starl stopped Wubbzy for an interview. "Wubbzy, you're a star!" the reporter said. "Everyone loves you. How do you feel?"

"I feel great," Wubbzy said. "I made three new friends and I got to go to Wuzzlewood with my best friends, Widget, Walden, and Daizy!"

"That's terrific," the reporter said. "One last question: What are you going to do now that you're famous?"

"Well, I've already been to Wackyworld!" Wubbzy giggled. "I had a great time in Wuzzlewood, too," he continued. "But you know what? I love being home with my friends. Wuzzleburg, here we come!"

Wubbzy and the Wubb Girlz Scrapbook
From Wuzzleburg to Wuzzlewood

Meeting the Wubb Girlz!

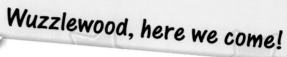

Wuzzlewood, here we come!

ckstage with the Wubb Girlz!

Shine and Wubbzy!

Walden and the Wubb Girlz
Shimmer and Sparkle!

Shine with Widget and Daizy!

It's good to be home!